The Moose Who Loved Noodles

Rachel Dutton

FIRST EDITION
ISBN: 9798534469455

www.RachelDutton.com

Every fall the park rangers invited all the animals to a big woodland party.

Boomer was very excited.
He had been looking
forward to it all year.

Boomer brought his specialty: a big salad of
tender young branches with maple leaves and slug-slime dressing.
He was *pretty* proud of it.

But at the party, he noticed that the humans were eating
something else. Something that smelled delicious!
But...everyone knows that moose don't eat noodles!

He chewed and chomped
on his sticks and leaves,
but he got splinters in his teeth,
and he wished for marinara sauce
instead of slug slime.

It was *terrible!*

His stomach grumbled.

He had an idea.

After he helped with the dishes,

Boomer hid under the rug until everyone went to sleep.

While the humans snoozed, he tiptoed down the hall...

Clop

Clop

Clop

and quickly crept over
the dining room table...

CRASH!

Clang!

Bang!

Boomer paused. Had he been a little noisy?
He decided he'd better hurry.

He flung open the refrigerator door,
and swooned at the sweet smell of pasta.

He gobbled and gulped and ate and ate and ATE!
The noodles were even better than Boomer had imagined!

He let out a very satisfied

BURP!!!

But Boomer

had been

a little noisy.

"What a messy moose!"
the park rangers cried,
and they asked
Boomer to leave.

Boomer knew his life would
never be complete without noodles,
so he thought of a better plan.

He donned the perfect disguise:
a big blue hat and a
dashing moose-tache,
and went to a restaurant.

He ordered lots
and lots
of noodles.

But when he bent over to gobble them up, his hat fell off! The people gasped so loudly that it hurt his sensitive ears.

"No animals in the restaurant!"
The chef yelled, and they pushed
Boomer rudely out the door.

Boomer felt very sad,
and very, very hungry.
He looked everywhere for stray
noodles, but the only thing he found
was a picture in a magazine.

Those noodles didn't taste good, but
they gave Boomer a fantastic idea!

He would go to Italy,
the land of pasta.

He got his passport,

put on his best pants,

and waited in lots of lines.

But the airline said he was too tall to fly.

And he didn't fit in a suitcase.

Boomer thought he would
never get his noodles.

sad and noodle-less.

He ate his yucky leaves and wandered around,

Then Boomer had an even better idea!

He bought flour and eggs
and oil...

He mixed and
kneaded and rolled...

He boiled and sniffed and tasted...

Until the noodles were perfect!

Boomer made so many noodles even *he*
couldn't eat them all!

He looked at the overflowing bowls, and felt...rather empty.

He wished he had someone to share them with.

Then he had his best idea EVER!

Boomer threw his own party,
and everyone came.
They ate spaghetti and
macaroni, and talked and danced,
and had a wonderful time.

But Boomer thought there
was still something missing…

Vegetables!

So he made his specialty,
maple leaf salad with
slug-slime dressing.

ABOUT THE AUTHOR

Rachel Dutton is a writer and artist, and general creative spirit.
She lives in Sherwood, Arkansas with her husband and dogs.
She does not have a pet moose, but she's open to the possiblity.

You can find more of her work at
RachelDutton.com

Made in the USA
Columbia, SC
08 March 2022